AF490819

Writer name: Kalliopi Kaplanidou. (in Greek Καλλιόπη Καπλανίδου.)

Copyright © 2012 All rights reserved.

Born in Greece.

Age: Born at 27-02-1976.

Για περισσότερες πληροφορίες για την συγγραφέα:
https://amazingcreationsshop.wixsite.com/kalliop isstories/about-in-greek

«In to a coma»

I could not stand my life anymore. How much I wanted to die! If you knew me then. I did not experience anything good. My parents kept having huge fights and they were getting their mad mood at me. I felt like they never loved me. The years passed and my soul was constantly abused. I was always dreaming of a better life, of a prince coming and taking me away, that was all I was thinking every moment......

I slept too early to make sure I will not witness them. Fate had heard the voice of my soul. I could not imagine how fate will give me what I was protesting for and asking for ....

...... So one day I found myself sitting in the back seat of my parents' car. Suddenly I felt a terror I saw nothing and then darkness. A car accident, everyone came out with minor injuries but I was hurt. When help arrived, they could not find my body. The back door was open they assumed I was thrown out of the car somehow. I had not opened the door. Almost 24 hours passed for them to find me. I was found by a doctor on the side of the road very far from the accident. They considered it an inexplicable fact but they did not care about it all they cared about was my health.

No one ever wondered how I was found there; I was in a coma and in a miserable state with many injuries. The doctor who had found me was in charge of a clinic for severe injuries and wanted me to be treated there without money. So it happened. On the other hand, I opened my eyes and felt a pain all over my body and then I was in a place new to me or so I thought. My God, where was I? Everything was new to me and yet I felt that everything was familiar to me. I did not have time to think of anything else because a young man was approaching me and talking to me as if he knew me.

- *«What are you doing here I was looking everywhere for you»* he told me, *« come on lets go »*. I followed him, I do know him I thought but then I know him, I know his name, I have feelings for this man. How is that possible I also feel like I don't know him I just meet him.

I began to fill with various memories of what I was seeing. I had begun to believe that I belong there; I just lost it for a while.

- *«You look at everything around you so strangely, as if you were seeing them for the first time»* he told me and made me come back from the thoughts I was lost in.
- *«"I'm fine" I replied "I just feel like a rock hit me in the head" I continued.*

Then I thought about what I answered and I did not understand it what was happening, because I felt so unnatural to answer him friendly but why he is my friend after all.

I did not know that all this might not be true. I started to think that something was going on in my mind, since I lived here, maybe I was sick with a flu and it affected my thinking.

As we kept walking everything, I saw evoked feelings of love, how much I loved what I was seeing it was all so familiar. The trees, the flowers, the smells, the sounds, the whole landscape. The white fence that was visible, the mansion that I saw from afar and that we approached, all even the large garden that existed around it. I knew everything, I had memories of everything!! I looked at them in awe. My attention was drawn to a huge dog that I saw running to me like crazy from the joy of seeing me. Without thinking, I knelt down and opened my arms to him. But I was afraid of dogs, and this one is big. I was now divided into two, two people, one reacted autonomously to everything because she knew all this and the other looked at the other self as a mere spectator and wondered about her movements and reactions and feelings thinking how is it possible. How do I know all this, am I losing it completely? I thought if all these feelings were not right I would not feel them will I.

On the other hand, he was such a handsome man, my heart immediately skips beats when I saw him even if it is the first time that I see him. My other self knew a lot about him, I thought I would learn them too.

I did not care about anything else. I wanted to escape from my life and now I was living another life. A wonderful life !! Filled with people who felt love for me and showed me affection. So I erased everything and believed that something would have happened to make me wonder about my familiar life, but I did not care anymore. I started to become one person as the hours passed and experience so much happiness.

We entered the mansion, I looked up and looked everywhere, and I felt the love that was in there. I saw as a dream myself living in there, running down the stairs to go down to the kitchen. The wonderful house! A figure overshadowed my light and I came out of seeing myself running to the kitchen. A man with an imposing face approached me with a smile and opened his arms to me. I felt so glad to see him. Without thinking, I ran to hug him and called him father! His hug was so tender and full of love. He was inspired me with safety and security I felt love for him. I had never felt like this about my parents. My memories told me that until now he had only offered me happiness. I was flooded with feelings unprecedented to me, joy, security, happiness, affection and not sadness and insecurity. So how can I not escape in to this life! It was exactly as I had been dreaming it will be all these year.

-     *«"Where were you my child you look so thoughtful. Is something wrong?".* My "Father" ask me
-     *«"I found her walking around absorbed in her thoughts, it seemed to me that she is a bit ... never mind and I asked her the same." John said.*

I replied "that I want to calm down a bit and I will be fine. I'm going to look around a bit and as soon as you have finished what you have to say come find me, I do not want to disturb you. I am not in the mood for serious discussions; I will leave and see you later."

I started wandering around inside the house, looking at the different places and then closing my eyes, I was taking in the energy of the room storing everything in my mind. It's like I would lose them and I never wanted to forget them. How calm and peaceful I felt!! I felt my soul so light. The house was large; I had wandered upstairs where it had a large room as a library, a living room and several other doors where the bathrooms and bedrooms were. All I saw were large rooms with large windows, so bright and with large balconies with great views! You could see the big garden and the distant houses of the city and the streets. I could not help but be enslaved by the sight of all this. I knew the same thing was happening in the other rooms. I had begun to forget the doubts I felt before. I stood in front of the window that was open; it was big in height and width, wide open with the white curtain on the side pulled. I looked outside feeling the breeze touch me as it passed me to enter this room. So much peace, so much happiness!

The silence was broken by John who came in and spoke to me.

- *«A! Here you are!»*

I turned and looked at him; I felt my heart beating fast, from his presence.

- *«The way you looked at me made me blush! This is the first time you look at me like that! " he told me.*

I looked at him full of wonder as he approached me and looked me in the eyes. I suggested we sit on the balcony and he accepted.

- *«"So much peace and quiet only here I feel it so strongly!" He told me,* since we were sitting in the comfortable armchairs that were on the balcony and he looked at me.

- *« Yes you are right, what did my father want you for? When did he call you? «I asked him because I did not remember if I had called him to come.*

- *«You call me to go out did you forget? Are you sure you are okay? Did you change your mind now that I reminded you about it? For the dance that takes place here in the city today»*

- «O! My god a thousand apologies! I do not know what is happening to me today. Moreover, of course our date is valid. I would never change my mind from doing something if we are going to be together on this. » God, I said it again the man blushed again! I thought. He touched my hand and looked me in the eyes, telling me.

- *«Whatever happens to you, I am here. And be sure that we will going to have a great time. I really do not mind that you forgot. The way you talk to me and look at me is enough for me. It will be dark soon, go get ready I will be waiting for you here.»*

When he touched my hand with his I almost fainted from anxiety. I think I was shaking, I got up and went inside, for a moment, I turned and looked at him and surprised I saw that he was looking at me with a style of admiration. I walked to my room, closed the door and stood short as my heart went like crazy. I felt like I was in love! I had to wear something beautiful and female; opening the closet, I saw many wonderful dresses, suits, outfits. I just glanced at them and my eye fell on a pink toilet, a lovely long dress with a soft silk fabric fitted on top and a little air on the rest of my body. I cannot describe it, whatever I say will be little. So I got ready in about 30 minutes, I did not want to make him wait long. I was anxious if he would like me until I reached him I had forgotten everything, every doubt, I was overwhelmed by the feelings I felt for him and the anxiety if he will find me beautiful.

- *«Wasn't it too late? Do we have any time left before we have to leave? "* I asked him and stood up next to him.

I was so anxious as I went in and as he turned and looked at me, he stood up and approached me and my heart trembled as he approached me more without saying anything. He took a look, he was amazed he grabbed my hand and I thought I would faint or tremble so much and he would understood how I was feeling, he kissed my hand telling me

«You look great!! So beautiful!! I feel flattered that I will accompany you !! We still have some time, why do you ask? "

- *"You make me blush by your admiration. I asked you about the time because I would like to sit here a little longer if you have no objection and talk, just like that»*

- *«I don't have a problem. Let us sit.»*

- *«It is wonderful here! I feel that one day I will leave from here and I will not come back. I want to remember these moments."* I told him and looked over to the city and the lights. He put his hand on my shoulder for a moment as a sign of support and tells me.

- *«It has been months since we met, but from our first meeting I felt that I have known you for years. I am lucky to have you by my side and to work with you, you are a wonderful person full of love for others and I felt this for the first time in my life. Wherever you go, I will not leave you alone we will be together and we will pass our hours as now! I promise. »*

I did not understand how that happened but that night I had opened my heart to him about my dreams, everything that I would like to do in my life. When he told me, it was time to go I was embarrassed because I did not know where we were going. I did not remember so I grabbed him by his cop so that he would not understand it. It was also an opportunity for me to let go the track I was feeling with him, and work for a while my mind, fortunately, he kept asking me about my dreams all night. We danced together, we both sat outside on the veranda, always the two of us. It was fantastic! He accompanied me to the house and when he said good night I went a little closer to him and looked him in the eyes wanting to tell him that I wanted him to kiss me. All the way back I held him by the arm and wanted him to stop hold me closer to him and kiss me. To feel his kisses and his hug. As soon as I approached him, he took me in his arms and kissed me. That kiss! A lasting kiss with so much passion, then he kissed my hair on the forehead and whispered to me.

- *«How surprised I was by the way you looked at me today, I will never forget those glances of yours. You filled my heart with happiness. Thank you for that! "And took a step back and left, looking at me one more time.*

I watched him leave with his car that he had left here because the driver had taken to us. In addition, on the way back we decided to go back on foot talking about our lives and dreams. I went up to my room full of joy with my soul feeling flooded by the offer of love, respect, pleasure and peace from the people I came in contact with all day. Something I never had before!

I woke up early in the morning at 7am I think. I will not forget how beautiful I felt, so much joy and happiness I had never felt this way ever before. As soon as I opened my eyes, I saw my room flooded with daylight. I got up, opened the windows and the coolness of the day came in. I had completely forgotten my other self, got dressed and quickly went down the stairs I went to the kitchen and met the cook who greeted me with a warm smile and made me breakfast without saying anything. I ate without thinking whether I liked them or not. I went out in the garden and saw the dog running at me, I played with him for quite some time at some point I looked up and saw my father figure looking at me with joy, apparently because he saw me so happy .

I had no worries in my mind, no unpleasant thoughts and memories! The wonderful thing is to have a mind without insecurities about anything !! I was free!

I walk in the garden, I went to the pond at the back of the garden, there I found, in the tree, a small place like a storehouse, I opened the door and saw two painting blocks and many pencils and erasers. How happy I was! I took a block and sat in the kiosk that was a few steps further down the trees, everything looked like a fairy tale and it was definitely artificial, I started painting the joy I felt. Until I heard a noise coming from somewhere, when I turned, I saw John coming towards me and the dog following him with crazy joy. I greeted him shaking my hand, left the pad and pencil next to me and got up to go to him. He was so happy! I hugged him and happily said.

- *«Good morning.» Let's go to the kiosk to sit", we sat side by side, with the dog sitting next to us. John saw the block and took it in his hands, looked at it and then looked at me*

- *«Such beautiful flowers, they shine like you, I did not know that you paint so beautifully. If I look into your eyes and observe them, I will see in the background hidden sadness! " He told me, I did not answer him, I looked away, taking my eyes off him.*

- *«Give me a painting that you will make only for me! " He told me maybe he wanted to make me stop feeling bad from his previous question.*

- *«I will fill the block with many and give it to you "I told him with joy, because he did not insist on answering him for before.*

I was saddened by his question. He did not touch me at all; he just looked at me with that strange style of his! Passion, he seemed amazed every time he saw me.

- *«"Let's have a great day," I told him somewhat abruptly.*

- *«Of course, what do you want us to do? I'm at your disposal.»*
- *«A ride with the horses maybe, or better to share the same horse, do you like horses? "After we can go on a picnic, generally walks but before all that I think I need, never mind" I replied.*
- *«I'm crazy about horses! Leave everything to me at the end of the day you will tell me your impressions. Please tell me what is it that you need.»*

I lower my gaze because I truly wanted to tell me kiss me that's what I need. He lifted my gaze putting his finger under my chin. I looked at him blushing and then look at his lips and he understood me. He blushed too. The dog came and try to link him on the face saving us from that moment. We laugh and I stood up that's how the day started. We walked side by side to each other and next to me from the other side was my dog. I followed him without knowing where he was going or if we had horses, but something made me say it, maybe seeing the size of the estate I thought they should have horses. He knew where he was going, I had not seen the whole garden yet, it was too big. Until we got to the stable, he was telling me funny things that had happened to him in his childhood. His face shone with joy, with happiness. I found myself in his arms, as he wanted to help me get on the horse. I looked him in the eyes and my whole body was asking for his kiss and his touch. He felt it too I'm sure of it that's why he took the courage to kiss me, at last. As he made this move, I hugged him passionately and as soon as he finished his kiss I kissed him and I or better I took him in my arms with a pull and held him tightly by grabbing him from his arms, as I was kissed him. I did not understand how I got this courage! Although at first I surprised him after he liked it I'm sure because he entered the game, he responded perfectly. I showed him that yesterday's kiss was not something accidental, there are feelings, I clear all his fears I believe. Because he told me

- *«Never leave me! I need you! My life has changed since you came! I'm not alone anymore, I'm happy!! I cannot imagine me away from you. Every day I wake up with your thought and when I will see you. To see if you are real or a wonderful dream that ended! I have not felt this way about anyone! From the first day I met you, I'm anxious if you will ever show me that you think of me too. I love you!! All this time I was in love with you and I waited, until that afternoon when you looked at me with passion and love. My heart went crazy! you finally felt something for me!»* and then he stopped talking, he was just looking at me a little scared, I was frozen with what he had told me, no one had told me that he loves me in such a way, no one! I looked at him in his eyes for as long as he was talking, seeing in his eyes the sincerity with which he said them. He loves me! Me! I believed that no one would ever love me because my parents had not shown me love. I answered him without hesitation, I did not want to worry him, he opened his soul to me and he was waiting for my reaction.

- *«Oh do not worry my sweetheart, I was not frightened by your words, the passion in your words is the proof that what you said you do feel them! No one has spoken to me so sincerely from his soul. No one has shown me that he loves me; confessing to me surprised me so much, my heart flies with joy now and if I knew that you are feeling like that, I would have approached you sooner. That afternoon something woke up inside me, as if I was sleeping and I just woke up seeing you for the first time. I felt so much for you. My heart was going crazy when I saw you outside my house and now that you hold my hands and look me in the eyes full of tenderness and passion .....! My heart beats like crazy! My heart wants to be in your arms again and to taste your kisses!»*

His face shone, a smile flooded all over his face. He took me in his arms and rested his face on my hair. I felt him enjoying the smell of my hair as I enjoyed the smell of his body and being in his arms. Without realizing it, I said, "Shall we go for a picnic than horse riding?" His response was a smile of happiness. We left the horse there and went to the car, got in and started driving. We were both in a sea of happiness. He made a stop at a mansion shop, made of wood, it was somewhere in the middle of our destination, after ten minutes he came out holding a big basket.

- *«Everything is ready»* he told me and looked at me smiling.

How happy he was! I put my hand on his and looked out of the car window, I felt like we had been together for years. I felt his hand caressing mine, I did not say anything to him, he said after a while

- *«We are here!»*

We got out of the car with smiles painted on our faces and we also felt embarrassed or guilty about something. He took the basket, opened the trunk and took the blanket. I thought maybe he always has a blanket with him just in case or he had gone on picnics before me. Of course, I did not tell him any of those thoughts, I did not want to embarrass him. Two steps further in the shade of a tree we laid the blanket and left the basket on. Opening it I could not believe my eyes, it had everything, everything! He saw my surprised look and his smile became brighter. He approached me, knelt in front of me on the blanket, I had just knelt on the blanket, he took my hand and held it and with fear in his voice, he asked me

- *«Does that mean that we are together now? That you are my girlfriend?»*

I could not believe what I was seeing! He was so modest!

- «YES "I told him out loud.» YES" I said to him again with passion.

He kissed my hand and held it with both hands. He turned to the basket, extended his hand and took out a box, opened it and turned it towards me. It had a wonderful pair of earrings inside, small and shiny.

- *«These are for my girl I got them before I came to see you. So if you told me that yesterday's kiss meant everything to you, I would give it to you. Something from me to be officially my girl.»*
- *«O!I adore them! I adore the thought too! It is my honor to wear them and never take them off! As long as I love you I will wear them!»*
- *«Did you say you love me; Did I hear well? " He told me and looked at me.*
- *«Yes !I am falling in love with you.»* I told him, he came to me; he hugged me giving me a kiss with so much passion! I responded with the same passion as a result we found ourselves lying on the blanket wrapped in each other's arms and the kisses followed one another. At one point, he just

looked at me as he was lying next to me with a part of his body above me.

- *«I Can't be dreaming of all this can I?»*
- *«No it is not a dream »* I said to him.

Lying next to each other, we began to tell our dreams for the future. We ate a little of the wonderful food in the basket, because we were not very hungry. We were living in a sea of happiness! We got in the car after we picked them up teasing each other as a reason to accidentally fall into each other's arms or by accidental touching each other. How happy I felt! Once we reached a point in the city leaving the countryside, we decided to walk to go for ice cream, regardless of the fact that it was not summer but early autumn. The cold had not started but when the sun was setting, you needed something more than a cardigan. We walked hand in hand spreading laughter from the jokes we were telling. He gave me flowers and a lovely teddy bear. We sat on the benches until the day started to pass, we looked at each other and the sadness came to our eyes for a while because of the fact that we had to part at some point. That's when he said to me.

- *«I do not want us to be separate, I'm afraid you will not be here when I wake up! I want us to be together!»*

I said to him.

- *«I do not want it either, but I do not intend to go anywhere, do not say that, come and stay at my house, father will be happy. Besides, he told me that he would be so happy if you will ever became his son-in-law. I did not want to embarrass you, you blushed.!»*
- *«If that's so, I accept, shall we go? I would love to be by your side for the rest of our lifes.»* he told me and we started for the return, we were not too far from home.

My father was so happy to see us together, he did not hide it, and he asked John to stay if he wants so he will not have to drive so far to go home. As if, he had read our thoughts! The joy I felt I cannot describe it. We spent many hours together on one of the wonderful balconies of the house with the wonderful view, talking until we fell asleep and each one went to his room. We went to our bedrooms together, first it was mine and then it was his. I opened the door and turned to look at him and said good night to him so sweetly, no he did not approach me enough to kiss me, just looked at me the same sweetly way and went to his door and before entering he looked at me again and smiled at me. The doors closed, I tried to sleep but I could not, I was so full with joy about what had happened. I wanted to go to his room to hug him, but I did not do it out of respect for my father, I knew he would not find out but I could not do it.

In the morning I got up, I did not have to worry for long about whether I would see him awake because I fell on him because I open my door and left my room in a hurried without looking around and I stumble on him. I felt so embarrass so I did not look at him when I told him timidly with a smile

- *«Good morning»*
- *«Good morning»* he answered me tenderly and hugged me to restrain me from losing my balance.
- *«I was waiting for you to wake up! I talked to your father and asked his permission so you can come with me if you would like it of course. I have to go for a few days, they need me in the office and ....»*
- *«Yes and of course I will come! Thank you for thinking of me.»*
- *«Go and pack what you need and we'll leave, they called me on my cell phone early in the morning that's the reason I got up so early»*
- *«I am on it I will see you in a while»*

I kissed him on the lips out of joy and went to get ready, I could not believe how quickly I prepared a bag with what I considered necessary. I went downstairs and saw him in the living room with my father, as it was natural I did not go unnoticed by my loud voice and my loud steps as I went down as fast as I could. I spoke to them as soon as I saw them.

- *«A   There you are! Here I am, I am not late am I ?! «They turned and looked at me; they both got up so they could help me with my bag.*

I have never met such kindness before in my life. How happy I was. Even for as long as it lasted it was worth it!

O! The days that followed were a dream come true! He treated me with so much tenderness, love, respect!! We stayed in a lovely apartment, they had a concierge and I had never seen something like that. Sometimes when we were out for dinner, it was just the two of us and sometimes they were business dinners. We would go for walks, he would buy me flowers and when he was at work he would send me messages on my cell phone writing how much he misses me, how he thinks of me, loves me and how he plans how we will spend the rest of the day together. He always held my hand with so much pride. No one ever felt proud to know me. Not even my parents! Without realizing it I helped him with his work, with the clients at dinners, with the office work he brought home some afternoons, giving him ideas and helping with his writing. The first two nights we did not make love, maybe he did not want me to feel that he wants to take advantage of me. I slept in his arms both nights. On the third night I prepared a romantic dinner in the apartment, with candles, music, I wore a sensual dress. When he came home surprised he saw all this, I told him that we would eat inside. We ate, I asked him to dance with me so I got up and offering him my hand he took my hand got up and we danced. As our lips joined, I let my hands and my body challenge him. His hand went to my back, to the naked part where the dress did not cover my back. I felt him being ecstatic but he felt embarrassed that I understood him. Then I started unbuttoning his shirt and kiss him on the neck and on his bare chest. I lowered my arms to open his belt and before I could he stop me then I told him

- *«A hot bath is waiting for you, I will rub your back, I really want to do it.»*
- *«Are you sure?»*
- *«Yes I am. I want to make love with you.»*

That's what happened. I will never forget that night everything was so perfect. The rest of the days went amazingly well. We were for each other the other half. We stayed together for twelve days. On the eighth day I started waking up from a dream, I woke up next to him scared because I saw a nightmare. I saw my life being nightmarish. Completely opposite to the one, I was living and I was so scared as I woke up. I woke him up and he took me in his arms and the fear was gone. I did not told him what I had seen. when we fell asleep after a while I woke up seeing the same dream and got up and went to his office and without realizing it I took a piece of paper and started writing what I saw and how I felt. Something I kept doing until the end.

- « My love I don't know what to do. I was so scared. *I don't know what that dreams means the one that I saw tonight but it is not good. I do not want to worry you but since we are together, you constantly tell me about your inexplicable fear that I will go away and you will lose me. For this reason, I cannot talk to you about the dream. However, I am writing to you about it and one day I will give it to you to read it, when I understand what this dream means. I hope it was only this one and I will never see another ....»*

Shortly before dawn, I went back to my bed and fell asleep. Nevertheless, the dreams that came were frightening although I did not wake up from fear this time I kept sleeping.

I felt him hug me and I opened my eyes, I shook his hands and I said "I LOVE YOU" I'm sure he understood that something had upset me and even if he did not tell me.

All day I felt a pain in my heart and all over my body. Luckily, we hadn't arranged anything, he went to work and I stayed in the apartment. I decided to draw something so that I could relax my mind. I started painting on the block I had taken with me, but I had left a block on the tree trunk for him in order to give it to him as I had promise him. After ten minutes when I started to relax, I started to see something like flashes of some kind. It was horrible, I saw myself crying with tears I felt a fear paralyzing me. I tried to open my eyes, to recover from the flashes but the flashes did not stop coming. This time I was seeing a big man came standing over me and yelling at me as I was curling up out of fear. Every time I tried to escape, another scene came in front of me and I was filled again with feelings and images. This time I saw that I wanted to die, I wanted it so much, I saw myself as a movie and on the other hand I felt like I was drowning, being oppressed, wanting to run away. My mind was filled with feelings of being humiliated, rejected, lack of love, I felt like I was a nothing. Without realizing it, I painted what I felt like I was hypnotized of some kind. They came and went like a wave, I immediately called my father, I wanted to hear him, and listening to his voice, I felt safe again. I tried to forget them by taking a shower, I got dressed, I put some make up I called John.

- *« My love do you have some free time to meet?»*
- *«Are you ok baby? I did not expect you to call me .....»*

- *«Don't worry I just got bored inside, I feel like I'm drowning I miss your presence»*
- *«Okay my love in fifteen minutes I will be there»*

Therefore, I went down to the entrance of the apartment building and had a conversation with the janitor.

- *«Hello, how do you do, I'm waiting for my husband and if I do not bother you I could keep you company until he comes. I felt lonely and bored alone ……………..»*

Although he found it a little strange, he accepted immediately

- *«My love! Hello Thanasis, shall we go? My love what were you doing at the entrance? Are you ok;»*
- *«I am, well, I was just so bored! Come on, don't look at me like that, believe me I am telling you the truth»*
- *«I love you, I love you very much»* he told me suddenly. I looked at him and saw the same fear in his eyes.
- *«Why do you feel afraid?»* I asked him feeling confused. Without hesitation he answered me immediately
- *«I'm afraid of losing you, I do not know why but I feel it and every time I see you something tells me that you will leave me»*

I looked at him in fear, a tear rolled from my eyes.

- *«I do not want to leave do not let me leave!»*

We both felt that something had started to happen without telling each other. The rest of the days were tragic. Returning to the apartment at some point, I fell asleep in his arms and the nightmare came again. I found myself watching as a spectator crying and suffering, I took part in the dream by having a dialogue with myself.

- *«why are you crying?»*
- *«Because no one loves me. I cannot take it anymore I do not deserve anything as a person. »*
- *«Why you say that you have a wonderful life»*
- *«You are in another world that's why you say what you say! You may have hid from reality but you will wake up at some point and then you will understand!»*
- *«NO!! It's not true! I will never wake up!!!....John where are you? Come to me, my dear, to prove to her that she is wrong. Where are you going? Do not leave, do not leave me alone, it is not true......where am I now? What am I doing in this*

hospital ?! Where are my clothes? Where are you why I cannot find you anywhere? John……………………»

Naturally I was shaken I felt paralyzed and I was talking as I open my eyes out loud *« Do not leave me John, why you left me in their hands why? »* Tears were running from my eyes non-stop without being able to recognize that I had woken up from the dream. Terrified, John hugged me and told me

-   *«Calm down, I am here! Do not be afraid, I will never leave you!»*

He held me in his arms and after a few minutes, I calm down. He did not ask me to tell him what had scared me so much. I looked at him and told him

-   *«I need to write what I feel without you reading it, I'm not ready to tell you yet I need to write it somewhere. When I'm ready I'll tell you,»* He said nothing, just looked at me and nodded yes.

He told me in his own way that he understood me. I started writing what I saw and felt. He just looked at me from afar without approaching me.

«O my god! I do not think I belong here! That girl came to my sleep again; it was me, I was crying, I was afraid for my future!! I felt that nothing would change and everything would remain the same. I will never escape. Why do I feel so much pain and abandonment? She told me that I would leave; I will wake up, how is it possible to live in a dream? Even if it is so, I do not want to leave! For God's sake in what kind of a horror do I live in?! I do not want to feel so much pain and humiliation no way! I saw it, it is so horrible there, I am so alone, no one loves me there!! I do not want to wake up and end up there! John, do not let me go back there alone to suffer!!!!»

I was left to look at what I had written for a few minutes, alone. John had gone to the bedroom and he was waiting for me. Entering the room, I looked at him carefully as if I was seeing him for the last time and he was just looking at me. I lay down next to him, put my head on his chest and told him

- *«I LOVE YOU!»* He stroked my hair telling me.

-   *«I cannot live away from you, my whole life is you!»*

I did not say anything to him, I just hugged him tightly and we fell asleep. This time I saw myself in a hospital dying unconscious.

Doctors talking, coming, and going, then I saw my lifeless body in a hospital room and many people crying. Then a doctor came and told them that there was no hope for me with such serious injuries. Who are those people that were there crying I wonder. Why am I there? What have happen to me? Suddenly a girl appeared next to me crying with tears. I approached her and told her

- *«Do not cry is not true, I am happy and alive, do not cry you are tearing my soul»* Then the girl stopped crying and looked around. I thought she would call for help; she seemed to be very scared. But even so she asked me
- *«Are you her spirit?»*
- *«No, I'm myself and you are in my dream now. I do not know you but I want you to know that I'm fine»*
- *«In your dream! No, it's not like that. I am in your reality, where you are is the dream»*
- *«**NO**!! You are lying! I am not leaving what I have no way! Nothing can make me leave, here I am happy!!»*

I felt like I was losing my dream but I kept seeing doctors running, I thought I was going to die for a moment. I opened my eyes, looked around the room for a moment and got up as quietly as I could . I went to the bathroom to wash my face, I looked in the mirror and thousands of memories came to my mind. I thought I was going crazy! I did not want to believe any of this. I said to myself that I do not want to go back even if that is the reality I do not care. I decided to go back to bed to John. I did not manage to take many steps and started seeing the flashes of images again. This time I was in a car and I was saying to myself that I did not want this life if something did not change and then suddenly a loud noise. The car turned upside down, for a moment I saw myself out of the car in blood. I could not bear what I was seeing and tried to find myself back away from those images. In this attempt, I fainted, because the shock was huge. While I was unconscious, I went back to the hospital I was in the body what I saw in the hospital. I panicked, *«what am I doing here I want to leave and go back»* I was saying to myself. Some came and talked to me in the hope of me hearing them. Listening to them, I got so mad I had bad feelings for them. *«They are big liars! Before they did not care about me and now they are showing compassion!»* I did not have time to say anything else because I had recovered and opening my eyes, I saw John talking to me terrified.

- 	«For *Goodness shake are you okay? Open your eyes my love, what happen?*»
- 	As soon as I open my eyes crying I told him « *Hold me tight!*»

I stayed in his arms without saying a word, without him asking me anything else. I felt his sorrow. I felt like I was leaving but I did not want to believe it. That night he stayed awake to look at me. I wanted to ask him why he is not surprised, how he keeps his composure but I was afraid of what he would tell me. If he knew something! At some point, it started to dawned and he fell asleep. I got up as slowly as I could but he was thrown upright.

- 	«*What happened are you ok?*»
- 	«*I'm fine I'll go to the bathroom and come back again*». He was so tired that he fell asleep immediately. *I went to his office to keep writing what had happened to me, feeling that I would not be able to tell him all that. « ....* *whatever brought me to you now it takes me away from you . I want you to remember me; only with you, I was happy. I am refusing to believe that you can be a dream and nothing more. Now I remember so much that I am frightened by these thoughts. Where there is the lifeless body that looks like me, people are bad and they treat me very unfairly and badly. I do not want to leave you even if it means I have to die in that hospital. A car accident brought me to your arms and to this world. That's what my mind tells me. I saw myself in a hospital half dead. Now I understand why I came to you and I do not want to wake up. You are the best thing that has happened to me in my life I want them all to be lies so I can stay with you. However, the most logical thing is for this happiness to be a dream. The love I feel for you is not a dream. Come and find me, if everything is a dream and I wake up I will refuse to live away from you. I will wait for you to come and if you do not come I will die so if you are a dream I will be with you again!! NO! I do not accept it! I look at you sleeping and I am afraid you will wake up and I will be gone! Come and find me wherever I am. I do not want to leave! If I had a sign that I will find you if I wake up .... I feel that the time is approaching when I will leave without*

wanting to. What will I become in that world without you?……………………………»

I felt my body hurting! I lay down next to him and looked at him, capturing in my mind his image his smell and how his body feels. I started to feel that something was pulling me back, back to that body. I got up, I could not close my eyes, I was so scared! At some point John woke up and came to me.

- *« What is wrong my love tell me.»*
- *«This is awful I do not want to go away from you.»*
- *«No, why go away from me.»* He turned my body so that I could look at him *« I cannot live away from you what are you saying?!»*
- *«I do not belong here god dammed! I remember them all! All ! We promised not to break up so tell me that you will come to find me, tell me!»*
- *«To come where? Where will you go; you are not a dream to me. Do not leave, I love you, I will not be able to stand being away from you !! How will my life be without you! I want you to become my wife and live together forever!!»*
- «This is not up to me I wish it was I'm sorry I'm very sorry! Hold me for as long as it lasts.»

The pain intensified and I started to curl up crying and shouting.

- *«No I do not want to leave …»*

I felt lost and then darkness. When I opened my eyes, I was in a hospital I saw a white room I could not move as much as I tried. Tears began to fall from my eyes as I thought « no it is not true I am not here! I cannot be here NO!» A doctor and a nurse came in and stood over me.

- *«You finally woke up! Do not be afraid, do not cry»*

I was not crying from fear of being there but for losing John. I did not talk to anyone because I did not care about anyone else. I had no good memories of anyone. On the other hand, the doctor claimed that I could not speak because of the injuries and that maybe in a few days I would be able to. Several people started coming, the room was full of people but I was not looking at any of them. I always looked out the window and a tear left every now and then. I did not pay attention to anyone. I was trying to dream of him to get lost in my memories of him.

- *«Doctor why she is like that?»*

- *«Maybe her mind is still somewhere else. Otherwise, the other version will be that she does not want to recover although I do not think so. Let's not forget how serious the injuries were we do not know their effects yet»*

A week passed and then the doctor began to suspect me since I looked at him here and there when he came in. He thought that something serious had happened and I did not want to get well. When I saw my parents, my heartbeat went up threateningly and this was evident in the machines that had me connected. I did not accept being touched by them I pulled my hands and cried. I cried because I did not believe that fate chose them to be here to continue living in this unjust life instead of being with him. At some point my nerves broke. I could not bear to see them I was screaming and my pulse was falling to the point that I was in danger of falling into a coma. They took them all out when that was happening.

- *« Calm down they are gone if you do not want to see them they will not come back I promise you that. As long as you promise me that you will start eating and talking»* I nodded yes. The next day no one had come, finally! Only the doctor together with a psychologist.

- *«Good morning . You see I kept our agreement. It took me a few days to understand why you react this way but now I know. How bad a life do you have to have to react like that? Not to want your parents! Do not turn the other way; all I ask of you is to participate in your recovery. You should start kinesiotherapy you have been in a coma for about four months and in a very bad condition. Here is another doctor and he will be like your friend, you will talk together, he is a psychologist and a good friend of mine»*

I looked at them with sorrow in my soul and in my eyes. If that would be the only way not to have visitors from my old life, I was willing to do it. I said to him «Fine». He looked at me surprised and happy because he saw me responding. He left and the psychologist stayed.

- *«I am Joa, tell me, why did you choose this way?… ..To look out the window constantly?»*

I looked at him in an ironic style because he would not understand me. He did not stop.

- *«Why not try to get well so you can get out. Whoever you expect to see will not be able to see you from here.»*

I looked at him sharply and told him.

- *«You know nothing about my life that 's why you're talking. I do not care about anything anymore from the moment I woke up everything was lost. My happiness was left behind in another life!»*
- *«What do you mean? While you were in a coma did you live somewhere else to another life ?! Interesting! No, I did not want to make you angry. Calm down, we'll talk about that again another time»*

He was finally gone! Alone at least! When I was, alone I could dream what I had experienced with John. Unfortunately, I had to start kinesiotherapy so I would not be alone for many hours. I did what I was asked to do in these exercises. I did not put too much pressure; there was not any big problems to deal with. They did not know that I was living a life when I was in to that comma even if it was a fantasy one and that helped me to avoid having problems now. Fortunately, the process took five days. During these five days, the psychologist came two or three times a day.

- *«You done with the exercises for the day, tell me what would you like to do that please you?»*
- *«A drawing pad, pencils and eraser.»*

I spoke to him in a few words and sharply I did not say anything more to him. I had no visits; I started painting and generally started to calm down. My heart was starting to bends. I was painting non-stop even at lunchtime. I started walking to the dining room but I was always looking out the window. I did not stop hoping that at some point I would see him coming. I had not yet begun to answer the doctor's questions.

- *« We need to start talking, don't forget that. Tell me why you refuse to speak»*
- *«Tell you what? About my life?!»*
- *«Yes it would not be a bad start. Do not look out the window I am still speaking to you! Why don't you want them? Your parents. "*
- *«Parents! All they care about is arguing and cursing. They do not care about anything else. That says it all»*

- *« I do not think that says everything. Tell me details you will feel better. I see you do not answer me well it does not matter. At least you started trying. We will talk tomorrow.»*

Without realizing it, I murmured something and he heard it.

- *«If you do not come and find me soon I will die»*

He asked me but I did not answer. Therefore, he left and came much later when I was sitting in a chair by the window painting. I did not hear him entering, only when he came and sat next to me.

- *«I see that you paint beautiful and happy things, but why do not you feel the same?»*

- *«Because I did not want to wake up !!! I was happy for the first time in my life where I was!!»* I shouted at him and got up throwing the block down and approached the window looking out.

- *«Who are you waiting for to come? Is it someone you met where you were?»*

I looked at him but did not speak to him. A tear dropped. I was ready to cry as the bellow words escaped me.

- *«I feel so alone, I was always alone here. You will not understand whatever I tell you»* He approached me and offered me his hug. *«It is not the same as his nothing is worth away from him»* and I pull away. I cried incessantly I went and perched on the bed and he left.

The next day that he came

- *«Yesterday I did not want to hurt you… .tell me what you lived while you were in a coma, please..»*

- *«I was happy !! They loved me! ! Why did you wake me up why? Why did you let me be happy? There I did not remember how bad my life is here!»*

- *«Tell me how ugly it is that's what I'm asking you!»*

- *«You will not understand because you did not live like me! By telling, they will not go away it will only make me hurt more. Why do it? Talking about them will not change how I live.»*

- *«Don't stop talking. Not again!»* I turn away and looked out the window.

………….……... On the other hand, from John's point of view it all started like this.

- *«I agree to talk about it because I want to remember every moment as proof that I am not crazy. I lived the most beautiful dream of my life! It all started that night, when I fell asleep I had wonderful moments. I was somewhere else but I knew the places there! They were so familiar to me! How was this possible? And then I saw an apparition, an angel, I felt the thunderous love in a dream! I was not so sure if it was just a dream. Because I still remember her form as clearly as back there. I felt and still feel love crazy in love with her. I had seen such a beautiful woman. She was there and she looked as if she was lost, as I approached her, I began to have memories of her and me together. How odd! Even now, it is so strange. I accompanied her to her house as naturally as if I was living there. I had a wonderful time with her. She looked at me in the eye at some point with a look of love and I felt lost in happiness and embarrassment. There were feelings in her eyes for me, I thought of love, now I know it was love. I was speechless! The love I felt for her from the moment I saw her was constantly growing. I was madly in love and I still am. My heart filled with joy and somehow I told her. I did not want to wake up! All day I was looking forward to the night to see if I would see her again. ……… ..I did not believe it, when I fell asleep early and saw her waiting for me!! I was lost in her eyes every time she looked at me. I felt my heart beating so fast! I saw her standing in front of the window the breeze was taking her hair it was like a dream. So beautiful! Oh my god! Every time I fell asleep and saw her I forgot my life and lived another life with new memories. Somewhere I remembered that it was a dream when I was with her. With her, I was calm, peace and joy filled my soul. When she showed me that she also cares about me it was a moment that I will never forget! I felt blush by the way she looked at me. I could not bear it and I touched her hand looking her in the eyes. I did not care that I saw her only in my dreams. I could not be angry with her ever. I want to protect her, never say no to her about anything. To be her friend and for her to be able to open her soul to me. Yes, even now I feel the same as then. She had forgotten our appointment once; I did not care about that I could not take my eyes off her. I looked at her wherever she went until I could not see her she was so beautiful! I wondered if it was a dream. I wish it weren't, that's what I was saying to myself. My life was full of her presence... ..I had told her how lucky I felt to have her near me. I could not imagine my life without her! I opened my heart to her as she did with me. I wanted to hold her hand to kiss her she was holding me by the arm and we were walking I felt so proud to have her by my side. I was afraid she might be scared if I kiss her, I did not know how to do it. I found the courage to kiss her. I did not want to do something that she did not want to do. I can still feel her lips on mine. This is how I was felling even after I woke up her lips on mine my love for her. It was impossible for me to believe that I can see her only in my dreams at night. I was wondering what was wrong with me and still do. That was when I got her a gift as I was going to work when I realized it; I thought I would probably have lost it if I thought I could give it to her in my dream. And then I decided to take a risk. And yes, I gave it to her! When I woke up, I acted like crazy of joy I did not know what to think. How did she get it if it was a dream this proves that it is not a dream. I was holding in my hands the empty box and the gift was missing. I thought of telling someone but to whom? I was ashamed to say it. The same day I decided not to wake up, I did not want to lose her. I did not put an alarm to wake up in time for work. She's my girlfriend I was thinking. I asked her to come with me and when I woke up I saw her next to me!!! I thought it was a dream, but I was wrong. Everything was wonderful my friends saw her she slept in my arms we made love!! I had never felt so good in my life. I was watching her sleep at night because I was afraid I might fall asleep and wake up and she will not be there. I could not get enough of her! She would come to my work and help me. I was wrong it was never a dream. After a while, she started not feeling well something was happening to her. I felt that I would lose her! She kept having nightmares! I did not dare to ask her I did not want to know! One time she fainted! I heard her, I ran to her, I had her in my arms and I shouted 'I do not want to lose her! My God, do not take her from me! 'And yet she was gone when I woke up she was not there! Why !? She had disappeared no I do not accept it! I never accept that she is gone! It happened what I was afraid of! I woke up and you were not next to me why, why did you leave we were so happy why? !!!! Were you real? Or were you of my imagination? How will I live away from you, you are my whole life why did you leave? I LOVE YOU!!!! Those were the words I shouted and filled my eyes with tears. Two days passed without me going out and trying not to think at all about anything. I wanted to die; nothing made sense to me anymore. I have been waiting for her all my life I live for her! I shouted to her, "where are you now that I need you!" I had to find out if she even existed; it was all I had left to do. I had to go to the places we went together, to ask my friends if they had seen us together. Like crazy, I was asking my friends if you could see how they were looking at me! «What is happening to you John why do you ask if I saw you with her? But of course we saw you, you are so lucky why what happen?» As soon as I got this kind of answer, I left without saying a word, like a mad man. Then I had to look to find out if that house she lived in existed. I remembered the route very clearly yes, there it was! To my great surprise, it was there, like a fool I was looking at it from afar from inside the car for a long time without daring to approach, to knock on the door. I was so scared of what I would find. If it was an empty, house what then? If she opened would she remember me what will, she tell me when she will see me? I could not just leave I got out of the car and went to the entrance. There was no sign of life in the yard everything looked abandon I started to worry. It looked abandoned for years. I knocked on the door of the house and found it open. However, there was no one and yet I saw her as if we had never left from there. My memories were so vivid, I saw her form everywhere and I followed her, but I quickly realized what all I was seeing are my memories. I went to her room and opened her closet; I was surprised to see her clothes there! Everything she had taken with her to my apartment was there!!! Her perfume was on her clothes, I took one of her clothes in my arms and smelled it, and it was as if I had her in my arms. It took me a long time to stop living with the memories and come together realizing how strange it was that her clothes were there. The clothes were freshly washed no trace of dust how was that possible? There was no one there the house seemed to be uninhabited for a long time spiders dust the covered furniture. I just felt a strange feeling that whatever magic had passed through here whatever it was that united us it had not been many hours since it was gone. The open doors the house that was unguarded without having been broken into how is that possible?!?! I spent many hours wandering around the rooms and chasing her figure. Desperately I sat on the floor and tears washed down my face until I remembered the kiosk, the painting block she would give me. I quickly went down the stairs and ran to the tree there I saw the block it was full of paintings with my face. I did not know how to feel it. Joy because you exist you are not a dream but then what have happened ?! I had lost it !! How is all this explained? Are you hiding where will I find you? I had to find out who owns this house. I found a detective and asked him to find out about this house as soon as he can. I waited for three hours and they seemed like centuries. He came:*

- *«What I discovered is very strange; the house belongs to a very rich man who had a daughter who died. For the rest of his life he searched to find the duplicate of his daughter to whom he had left everything. Nobody knows if he ever found her, he has been dead for 7 years. However, mysterious things happened a few nights ago, say the locals. They say they saw people living in the house a young couple and the deceased!! A man who was coming and going by car and the girl was his daughter!! They were not ghosts because they saw them at the city dance and talked to them. Moreover, one day all of a sudden they all disappeared! No one has managed to get through the courtyard door! The man is said to have come again and it is you! I showed them your photo as you asked me. The house maintain by yourself for seven whole years! Some even told me that they believe that he is waiting for her the girl that the old man was looking for!!..............»*

I could not bear it I lost my balance feeling as if I was losing the ground under my feet. I was dizzy, I held by my desk I sat in the chair and did not speak. I looked at him who was looking at me and I just said thank you to him. As soon as he left, I ran to the toilet and washed my face I looked in the mirror I was pale. I was at work I went back to my office and stayed there until nightfall looking out the window. I had her block on my desk for a moment my gaze fell on it and stayed there. I saw her as a memory, painting with that wonderful smile and then I remembered that she was painting in my apartment too. I had seen her many times, so maybe they were still there; this thought made me run home. As soon as I entered, I headed to the office where I had seen her sit so many times. I was right all were there, another block and some notes. For God's sake what is happening here ?! The paintings were so sad in some there was the figure of a man who terrified her I did not know who he might be. Even what she had written was full of sadness. I was so scared is it true or not I was telling myself. What should I believe! I was terrified that if everything was true, she had an accident, and she had such a bad life. I was terrified at the thought that she had returned there and was alone without wanting to be there. If I was a dream ? At that moment, I promised her that I would find her. We are both real! That is what I wanted to believe! Something higher had united us I knew I could not live away from her. I did not want to eat, to sleep, I cried, I wondered why, where is she now; I was asking God for help. I was desperate I was about to go crazy I looked at the blocks and the notes over and over again I shouted indignantly at her she knew she will leave why she did not leave me any information on how to find her.

Until I noticed something, a signature on one of her paintings with another name and surname !! I immediately got the detective no matter if it was early in the morning at that moment I was not thinking of anything else. Not to mention, he came after hours, fortunately the man came without being mad with me. My head was going to break a knot in my stomach finally the bell rang!

- *«Come on in»*
- *«Man you look like shit!»*
- *«I know. I called you here because I want you to find me a person the girl of the house who saw us together. Find out about her life I have a name and a surname for you look for*

an accident maybe the date is close to when the residents saw her at home.»

- *«That are more than enough. You tried to calm down a bit because you look like you are about to break down, I will call you when I have news. It will not take me long»*

He was gone and I could not bear to be home and wait. I thought about going to work maybe it would help me but even there I did not feel better.

«John! I am talking to you! Where is your mind? You are in your world! I have never seen you like this! You have been here for 3 hours and as many times, as I entered you did not hear me coming, you are immersed in your thoughts. What is happening to you? You have days to show and now that you are here you are not.»

«You are right; I was lost in my thoughts. 3 hours have passed really?! I have a serious problem leave me alone please!»

«Are you sure; I am leaving fine if you need anything .....»

2 days passed like a century. There was the same question in my mind, what I would find what would the truth be and when the phone would ring. With each ring of the phone, I ran like crazy and the frustration grew. At one point, he called me. The information were a lot the ones he found .When he finally came, my hands were shaking and I could not open the door.

«Come in»

«I must confess to you that you are involved in a very strange story! I found her because I looked for an accident on the date you told me and I found her! She is the girl who died and of course, she is her duplicator! The one the old man was looking for I cannot explain the rest except to make assumptions. Maybe the old man's spirit brought her here. What else to think! However, I have seen many strange things in so many years in this job so I believe in everything! The girl is in a clinic and refuses to recover. They have banned the visits of her relatives and parents !! She had a bad childhood. Here I have everything in detail photos of the girl excerpt from the newspaper and the clinic where she is. I did not see her because she does not go out in the yard at all. It's all here. What do you intend to do now?»

«So she is real! I did not imagine it! Thank you! I want to ask you one more favor I do not dare to go alone will you come with me? You are the only one who knows about all this.»

«Okay. I would also like to ask you a favor. I am preparing a book with my work and I would like you to tell me all about it and to include it as well.»

«Why not shall we go?»

So we started, our destination was quite far, first we passed by the neighborhood where she lived and then to the clinic ………..

I who was with him will continue telling you what happened. I took him to the clinic when we got out of the car I saw him standing still I thought maybe he had change his mind. However, no, we kept going we went in and he remained serious without speaking. A doctor saw us and asked us who we were looking for and I asked him to show us who was the doctor who was responsible for the girl. I explained to the doctor that I was not a journalist as I had told him but a detective and that I was representing the gentleman who was with me. He took over and told him:

«Doctor she is waiting for me if you tell her who I am there is no way she will not accept to see me»

He said nothing else. The doctor looked at us and led us to the place where the girl was. She was sitting on the edge of the room with such a sad look on her face that it broke your heart seeing her. He recognized her immediately his eyes shone! He whispered «I have never seen her so sad!» He approached her touched her on the shoulder and she was scared turned and saw him from her expression I thought she would faint. She was motionless surprised then fell into his arms crying. I approached a little and heard her say to him

«You came, you were not a dream! You found me! How scared I was! You are finally here! You will take me away from here..!»

He held her face with his hands and kissed her.

What happened next is even better. She explained to the doctor that she thought she would never see him again and that is why she did not want to live. But now he does not have to worry he can let her go. I also intervened, explaining in a few words the incredible story as I write it to you. The story does not end here. They asked me to find out who owns that house now so they could buy it. And the strange events continued we found that the house and so many other things were written in her name. The old man had not had time to tell her that he had found her. I think the old man united them when she was in a coma in his world.

I asked them to tell me the whole story to add to my book with all the incredible stories I have solved.

This is an imaginary story.

ONOMA ΣΥΓΓΡΑΦΕΑ: Kalliopi Kaplanidou. Καλλιόπη Καπλανίδου.
Copyright © 2012
All rights reserved.
Γέννημά θρέμμα ελλάδάρα!
Γεννήθηκα στης 27-02-1976.
Για περισσότερες πληροφορίες για την συγγραφέα: https://amazingcreationsshop.wixsite.com/kalliopisstories/about-in-greek

I loved a criminal

Antigone - Come on in, sit down, let's get started. My name is Antigone; do you know why you are here?
Her- But of course! To sit here, I have to tell you everything. The judge imposes it; it is the only way to convince you that I knew nothing.
Antigone - Yes, that's right. I am a psychologist and I will listen to your story not to judge you if you are guilty or not but to make sure there is no psychological trauma inside you. Let's start, start talking to me.
Her- Ok, I will tell you how it all happened. It all started in that street, that morning... I do not remember dates. I could not imagine how important what I would see would be and how important role it will play in my life to keep the dates. For some unexplained reason I was there and I had to see what later cost me so much. No, I will not torment myself anymore with the 'why' I was there and saw what I saw.
Antigone - So, you do not feel anger, nor wronged in any way?

Her- No, it makes no sense anymore. I lived many years trapped in the 'whys' of life I learned my lesson. I was probably ready to take this test of life. A little wronged, maybe, but I learned my mistakes at a hard price. Before I meet him of course, so I do not have to tell you that. Anyway, every obstacle comes for our own good. That morning my friend forced me to go with her to a chore she had, but with the various unexplained circumstances, we found ourselves on the wrong street. I felt upset because I went by force and we got lost on top. As we were, looking around to see where we were something made me look back and I was staring at the road without being able to resist. Suddenly I saw a car stand out it turned very fast from the corner and I stayed there to look at its license plates. They were immediately etched in my memory; in no other case would I be interested in such a thing. My friend spoke to me and I was spooked because I was completely lost in the moment and she asked me what was I looking so persistently but I did not give her any answer I just looking at her confused by my act. At that moment, we heard sirens and saw a police car turning from the same corner. We wondered about it but did not pay more attention to it we continued to walk for about 15 minutes. At some point, my friend stopped staring at a shop window while I was standing a little further and before I could understand it, a man fell on me. When I recovered from my terror, I looked at him and I was speechless. He was a very handsome man, at least for me, so well dressed and with such a good fit body! I felt lucky that he fell on me! He apologized, looked at me and told me how glad he was that he fell on me and so it became the occasion to meet such a beautiful woman like me. Oh, I was so flattered! He was so handsome! He kissed my hand and at that moment, two big men approached and asked him if he was okay and told him they had to move on. To my surprise, he told them to go on their own and not to bother him. They did not like it but retreated a little further.

Antigone - What did you think of them?

Her - That they are his friends. Although something told me how mysterious they looked, I did not care tho. I was thinking of him. He asked me to let him take me out, for a coffee or dinner or whatever I wanted. As he told me, he would like to do it now but his friends and turned to them and looked at them. Meaning he could not do it now because he was not alone.

Antigone -Did you say yes?

Her - Who would say no! I was not in a relationship and I needed to flirt at that time, my self-esteem was down and his flirt it seemed like a dream to me at that moment. We made an appointment to meet somewhere, I may have been excited but I was not stupid to accept his invitation to come pick me up and show him where I live or get in to a stranger's car. And I did not want to show him that I was crazy about him. Therefore, that is how our first meeting happened. He was waiting for me alone with expensive and at the same time very modern outfit holding a rose in his hand. A white one not a red one. I do not like red ones but he did not know that. As I was crossing, the road I saw him! He had seen me and he was smiling at me, he looked so happy that he saw me that made a great impression on me! Of course, this boosted my morale.

When I approached him he kissed my hand, he gave me the flower with so much joy explaining that I deserve every move of a gentleman and I did not have to be hesitant because he would treat me like a gentleman. I smiled at him, that's all I did. He asked me if he could choose a place or if I had a particular preference. I was thinking how lucky I was to choose to wear the right clothes in relation to his own outfit. I told him he could decide so he could have a chance to show me how much of a gentleman he is so I don't have to worry! I do not know how I said that! I felt so different being with him!

Antigone - Different in what way?

Her - I felt like a woman. I felt like I was becoming an independent dynamic woman who was not afraid to talk to him in a cold and honestly way, about what she was thinking! Something I always dreamed of becoming! And not a frightened 25 year old girl who still tolerates paying for the mistakes of others from their wrong choices and letting them direct her life without respecting her!

Antigone - I see an indignation towards some, but to whom?

Her - Let's leave it like this, after all my life has change. He just came into my life at the right time, the moment I couldn't take it anymore, I wanted to leave and be alone away from everyone and everything. I wanted to find a job that I like and pursue my dreams. Making my own choices, my own mistakes learning from them without protest because it would be my own mistakes.

That's what he did for me, he spread my wings for me! He proved to me how capable I always was, I just did not know it. He dispelled all my phobias and raised my self-esteem (her gaze was scattered around the room as she looked around for a moment. It is a room full of dark color items, red colors on the armchairs and curtains; a table near to the wall, the room has very modern and simply decorated items everywhere. Light came in through the large window behind where the doctor was sitting. From the outside, the building looked like a school building. She lowered her gaze and continued to narrate as she lived again every moment she is saying.) He took me to a stylish cafe the ones that are so expensive that you might pay three times as much for a coffee. We walked there. Every now and then, he would put his hand on my back when he wanted to warn me about the sidewalk, the puddle or a hurried passerby. He certainly had never done this before! I mean not to take the car but wait in front of a shop window …………… ..Made me laugh constantly commenting in a humor away about the people passing in front of me, on the imperfections of the sidewalks. He joked about these situations! The so narrow streets that the oncoming car was forced to pass, for the ones parked on the sidewalk, the crazy ones who were walking and talking! He was having an amazing sense of humor! I loved the fact that he was watching out if someone bothered me or made me stumble!!

It was as if I had known him for years, the shame was gone and I was talking to him as if he were my best friend and he was very comfortable with me, so I asked him if he was comfortable with everyone he knew, giving them the opportunity to feel like they had known him for years. Then he stopped moving, he looked me in the eyes, he held my hand, I had never felt like this in my life! Oh my god! I thought it was like looking into the eyes of a man in love! He looked at me with such tenderness, so.. How to describe it, he was like he was enchanted by me, no matter how selfish it sounds. I had fallen in love with him. Those eyes, the way he was looking at me !! ……he looked at me and he answered me with a serious look 'NO"! No one has ever made him feel that way in his life and that only I take out this piece of his character. My purity, the honest way I talk to him without being afraid of him or letting him feel that whatever he says I will accept it as it is. I make him be afraid that I might refuse or not be satisfied with his proposals and that filled him with life. However, the most important thing he told me is how he feels when he is next to me. The energy I emit... a peace, hope and vitality that's what he told me. He believed that he could trust me with his life, to change his life for the better. If only he knew, I would betray him in the end. He said it so seriously that it scared me! It came out of his soul! He believed what he was saying! He would not want to lose me from his life in any way.

Antigone - Didn't you find it a bit strange for him to tell you all this so quickly, without knowing you?

Her - But of course! However, you were not there to see through his eyes what I saw! Besides, I had such a great need to be flirted and flattered ..... It was as if he was confessing his love to me at that moment, it must have been very difficult for him to remain completely uncovered and open his heart. You know how men are, since it is so difficult for men to open their hearts, he was taking a huge risk with me at that moment don't you think? (She did not want to interrupt her, her eyes were shining, the doctor could understand the feelings she was feeling and the fact that she was living the moments she was telling her. She nodded to her, let her tell her story she could not speak she was so surprised listening to how she was telling her story. Although she did not believe in energies and stuff like that, she felt it; she felt the energy she emits, all her feeling were all around her. She felt it from the moment that the door of her office opened and she had entered. She feels the sadness, the joy, the passion in her words as she speaks. She feels she is experiencing everything that she is telling her she knows that she is telling the truth. It is an amazing experience for the doctor.)

Her - I was speechless, flattered and we continued to walk until we arrived. It was a very stylish cafe with glass all around it a corner two floors place. You could see everywhere and almost everyone if you were waiting for someone, he would definitely be the first to see you before they even come in. The seats were armchair-style in beige color. Before I had the change to pull the seat, he had done it!! Although the waiter was ready to do it, he told him not to. It gave us a few minutes to decide what we would get. I was so flattered! of course I told him that for the first time in my life I am feeling so beautiful and that was the reason I had lost my speech, I asked him to forgive me and he smiled at me and said "you deserve it!». You make others feel so comfortable and so confident next to you that it is impossible for them to resist and behave differently". After that I was melting! I could not bear not to say it and like stupid I told him that until now I had not been treated that good how it is, possible that he was feeling that way for me. Even now I can not believe it. Even now! He was and is the only person who until now has treated me with such respect and appreciation. I had impressed him with what I had told him and he answered me with such tenderness " How is this possible, if you think you will see that you are wrong, maybe because of the age of your friends they do not know how to show it, but they will have in some point right!? »

"Maybe you are right," I told him, I did not continue, the pain had taken over my heart, and he had seen it. The waiter came and we ordered, he continued to talk to me "I see so much pain in your eyes it is possible that you have been hurt so much! Sorry I brought the pain to the surface, I feel my heart pounding…"He took my hand as a statement of support. He was sitting across from me and got up to sit next to me with the pain written in his eyes! For me at that moment he was the first person to appreciate me like that and see who I am! You will never be able to understand it! That's why I loved him! I told him I did not want to spoil his night or remember all that and we changed the subject.

Antigone - Would you like to talk about it, about the pain you felt, do you still feel it? After all, you are here; you can use your time here and will stay between us.

Her - No thanks. This is over now. There is no such pain, he drove it away …….

Antigone -Do you still love him?

Her - I do not know if I still love him, I'm so confused now …

Antigone - Let's continue unless you want to take a break.

Her - No, I am fine. (She looked up and continued to remember, her eyes are having the same radiance.) We matched immediately! We laughed, he told me jokes, and it was wonderful! We did not want the time to pass, he made me shine with joy, but he shone too! He told me endless compliments, who could resist…. The afternoon was over and it was evening, we had ordered two more times because we were there for so many hours. So I said good night to him but he insisted on taking me back. I told him that if he wanted it so much, he could accompany me on the bus and he had no objections!

Antigone - Did he take you to your house by taking the same bus ?!

Her - Yes!! That had enchanted me! He had win me over! Who would do that? He told me he wanted to meet again tomorrow and I accepted immediately! So we met again. This time he was in his car and we met a little further from my house.... He shone and smiled at me! I got in the car and looked at him, how much I wanted to kiss him, but I did not, he took me for a picnic. I had never had a picnic before; the radio was playing music as he drove us to the countryside.

Antigone - How was his outfit, his car? Did not all that show that he was rich? Was there anything to make you suspect him?

Her - Not very rich, he had an expensive car but nothing showed that he had too much money he was discreet. I saw the city moving away and images of nature appearing everywhere. I did not know where he was taking me, after all, even if he told me, I would not know, I did not move around much to know the areas. I was not talking, I was just enjoying the view and the happiness that my soul felt about the fact that I would spend another afternoon with him. I looked at him without him looking at me and wondered if he was real or part of my imagination. However, I do not care I thought, I would enjoy the joy and happiness and I looked out the window. At some point, he touched my hand with his, I turned to look at him and he smiled at me he had a look of happiness because he was just with me! I could not believe that someone could feel so happy because I was with him!

Antigone - Again, you express feelings of inferiority why? Why did you think of yourself that way?

Her - Because! Simply because until then no one had treated me like him .... He asked me if I liked the landscape and I told him that I was crazy about it. On our way we passed many villas, we were on the road for a long time until we reached an oasis! The owners of the villas built the park, I assumed he would be a businessperson or he would definitely get a very good salary to be able to be there. So he opened the door for me before I could do it myself and went to take out the basket he had bought full of delicacies! I thought I was living in a script of a movie; I was excited about this experience. He asked me to follow him and I looked around without being able to believe in the beauty I was seeing. How well they maintained the park, benches, tables, fountains, swings in the center and heart-shaped benches carved everywhere even behind the trees, some of which were covered in a way so couples to sit there and kiss. The park did not have many people. We put the basket on one of the tables that

was behind a tree to have more privace, we laid a blanket on the grass, and it was a wonderful spring day. As I helped him I did not stop looking at him, I did not want to lose any image of him. I want to store it all in my memory. I did not want to forget how perfect everything was, his kindness.... (Her gaze wandered into the room without looking around. She was lost in the moments living them again in her mind. Absolute silence all that could be heard was her voice.)We started taking out various wonderful dishes such as fruits, canapés, cheese pies, cookies and many more very meticulously made. He told me that they made it for him and he hopes that I will like them but also he hoped I was very hungry! We sat, enchanted by nature and romance, I could not bear not to open my soul to him. I believed that, perhaps, I had found my man and if that's so why not open my heart to him, show him who I am. My face would have taken a serious look while I was thinking about all that because I suddenly felt my hand resting on his hand and I was a little spooked because I got out of my thoughts by his touch. He asked me what I was thinking about and he hoped it was not something bad and his face suddenly became serious and he asked me to go near him. I sat next to him and he hugged me, I felt so safe, it was not an erotic but friendly, compassionate hug. I looked up at the sky and without realizing it, I had told him "I am so lonely and scared; you will not like me if I let the fear and insecurity I feel overwhelm me". "Do not be so afraid, I want to know your dreams and your fears," he told me. "My dreams..", I said and stopped because a tear wanted to run down but I held back, even though he saw it. "I'm afraid I will never make my dreams come true, I'll be stuck here" I answered him. "What would you like to have in your life?" he asked me and I answered "Independent"! Financially, professionally, to live in my own apartment and live the experience of furnishing it without thinking about the money that will not be enough and how I will live without money. To be able to prove to myself that I am capable of doing it. To study what I want to learn, working out and so much more." He told me that I had found my vitality again, but for a while, he was still thinking. Without realizing it, I had told him all my dreams and he seemed happy his face was shining! I felt so good about myself because I saw him enjoy my company so much.
Antigone - Why do you say that?

Her - Because my mood was not good enough to help me make friends. To me he stood as a true friend and companion, he changed my life forever. I saw my craziest dreams come true! I could not imagine the end! Impossible to have understood who he was, I tell you again with me he was someone else! My hero.

Antigone - Do you think he loved you? Does he still love you?

Her - I have no right to question whether he loved me. Yes, he loved me, how else can you explain that he gave me a life without asking something in return! How do you explain the fact that with me he was someone other than the one you all knew? Maybe he wanted to change his life when he met me I do not know that! I do not know how he feels about me now I will always feel guilty for what I did.

Antigone - Because he gave you everything and you betrayed him, no do not feel that way, you did the right thing.

Her - The right thing! ...... I wish it were that easy I would not change my action with anything .... I don't regret what I did don't worry about that. Nevertheless, he was perfect by me that will never change either.

Antigone - Lets continue ....

Her - Our relationship developed quickly and rapidly after that day... ..He bonded with me and I followed him as he directed my life at a fast pace without being able to realize the changes.

Antigone - Didn't you hear what was happening? From the TV, from somewhere..

Her - I did not watch TV, let alone the news, at that time my mind belonged somewhere else because I was in love. All I wanted was to be with him all the time.

Antigone - Do you feel wronged?

Her - Unjust? No! I lived something special! I saw my dreams one after the other come true even for a while, for as long as it lasted !! .I'm not ungrateful! I am grateful for what I experienced they gave me the courage and strength to continue my life. To hope and not to stop moving on! Back then I had reached the amen of my patience, I was so alone. I was not filled with what I had because I knew that my future could be different, better. I had just started to lose my courage and he came to give me wings. Do you enjoy working here in this moody building every day?

Antigone - You get used to it. But at least I do the job I like.

Her - So you see, I just lived in my daily life in a difficult job without many earnings, without a future. With the only hope that one day, everything will change. Now I live the life I always dreamed of. The change in my life started immediately the next day. He came to our appointment and told me "You do not need to work where you do anymore, not anymore, I want you to accept the opportunities I want to offer you and if you succeed with your value you will keep them." Of course, I was speechless and I stood there staring at him. On the one hand I did not want him to feel that I was taking advantage of him and on the other a whole life I prayed for someone to come and give me the opportunities to do what I dreamed of and I would put all my energy to prove that they were not given them to me unjustly. And now this was becoming a reality. He saw that I hesitated and grabbed my face in his hands telling me that I have to accept because he loves me and he cannot have so much and see me die slow in the life I do. In addition, he told me that I would do the same for him and he was right! I would do the same and I would want him to accept my help. I looked at him, my eyes watered and I nodded yes. He asked me to say it again because he did not understand what I said to him and crying I told him yes. He hugged me! As I was in his arms, I told him with tears running " Those are happy tears I do not believe that I will finally be able to feel that I am a worthy person doing something in my life. Working hard so that neither you nor God regret the opportunities you are giving me!! ". " You are a worthy person and you have to believe it, you are already."He told me.

He told me that he asked his friends to give me a change because he believed very much in my abilities! He took me to a very beautiful building, I went in and I could not stop looking around, I felt a shiver it was like in the movies. I was not anxious because of the admiration I felt for the building. We went up to the offices where his friends were, the building was empty, and he showed me all the spaces, the toilets, the cafeteria, the gym, the offices. He explained to me how they work here and then we entered the office of the 'leader' where his friend was waiting for us. We introduced ourselves, he was very kind, and in the end, he turned out to be a very simple and good person. They explained to me that they would pay for the training I would need to do and those lessons will happen here in some of the rooms that exist and that I would be able to go to the gym like those who work there and work as a secretary. I was over exited! From a difficult and dirty job that I was doing now, I would work in luxury! When we left and left the building, I hugged him and screamed, laughing and crying at the same time! He took me for a drink and there we discussed about the fact that I had to find an excuse to tell my family for how I got this job. And of course what I thought was very crazy but I told them in a very serious tone and they believed me.

Antigone - What did you tell them?

Her - Even that I need to say it to you... come on.... I told them that while I was drinking coffee with my friends I heard them say at the next table that they were looking for a good girl and ambitious to teach them the job because they were desperate with those who went and then I got up and apologized to them for bothering them but I heard what they were saying and that I want to try this position too. If I was not good for them, they could fire me! Of course, my family were confused, they did not know what to say but I did not have to go to mom's job ever again! Finally!!

Therefore, he came in the morning at 8:30. My family were at work already. He came to take me to a women's clothing store where he bought me the right clothes for the job. The company wanted to do it but he refused and paid for it himself.

At work, the environment was perfect, I filled my mind with optimism, generally positive things did not stop from happening to me and coincidences came one after the other!

Antigone - So you believe in things like that.

Her - Yes. Very much. I have read many books about trying to stop thinking in miserable ways because whatever you think that is what happens to you.

Antigone - What happened after?

Her - Within a month, my life was very different! I was very good at what I had to do at work, I helped the other girls when they had a workload and I became very lovable. They gave me private lessons every day and on Saturdays because I wanted to learn everything quickly. Each day we were having an appointment with him at the gym. I went earlier than everyone else at work did and I was putting flowers in all the offices before anyone arrived. I would go to work with one of the guards who passed by my house and sometimes he would come and we would have breakfast together somewhere near the office.

He often came to visit his friend and we ate lunch together and he would take me back to my house, the house with the office was quite far. At some point I do not know how this happened, in the same building they also had a book publishing department and the young man we were exchanging good morning asked me to read some pages of a novel and tell him my opinion about what he had written because he was stuck and did not know how to continue the chapter. I was very excited about this opportunity and when he came to pick me up; I told him all about it.

Her -You will not believe what opportunity has come!

Him - What?

Her - I was asked to read a novel and give my opinion! You know what that means! I have always dreamed of doing this, of helping to write or by correcting a book! It's amazing! Maybe... nothing in life happens like that, everything happens for a reason!

Him - I never thought about that, I like the way you think!

Her - The truth is that I write stories.

Him - Seriously! I want to read them!

Her - Therefore, I gave them to him my stories and after three days, I was invited to go downstairs where he was waiting for me along with many others. They liked the stories so much that they wanted to publish them in a book! So you understand that I owe him so much!

Antigone -Yes, but do not forget that he gave you the opportunities but you also had the skills to stand out!

Her – (She sighed) Yes maybe but it is ungrateful not to believe in him! I used as an excuse to say to my family on how I got to buy a house the book along with the fact that I helped my boss by choosing a share and he won a lot of money out of the stock market. The second one was not true but I had to say something. The truth was that he pay for it, when he took me to it I did not knew that it was for me. I loved it at first sight! It was perfectly furnished and I noticed that everything was as I had told him I would love to have in my house one day and there I realized that it was for me. So I left from my parents house without them wanting it. Nothing was holding me back in the life I lived before .....

Antigone - Did you live together?

Her - Yes, he was my first you know. So tender so gentlemanly ......

Antigone - Oops the phone, sorry for a moment. (She picks it up) I'm coming! I have to leave you for a while if you do not mind.

Her - No, go I will wait. (The door closes and she is left alone doing the following thoughts.)

Let me get up and go to the window behind the desk in the light that comes in. To see a little light in relation to the rest of the room, the view outside is so depressing too. I feel just like when I came, it is a lonely prison. Moreover, from outside when I came and stood for a while I felt how cold this place is, but I imagined that behind the windows there would be figures of patients looking outside and feeling so alone. What to wish for, being in a place like this one? All your hopes are frozen, even the huge trees with their branches and the silence that prevails fills your soul with loneliness. Ah, you are in a similar place, my love, but yours is in some prison, but I do not prefer to think that I prefer to think that I am telling you all this like one of my stories. I cannot help but remember our first time, you were so tender! It all started with a candlelit dinner at home, music .Even now I can still hear the music and feel the smells so vividly penetrating my senses. Dancing, kisses the chemistry that had been created, I unbuttoned your shirt and kissed you on the lips, on the neck, on your chest. You didn't have time to ask me why, I told you I want to make love, sweetheart you knew it was my first time and you made sure everything was perfect, thank you! You guided my hands as I took off your clothes and kissed you! ... ..When I took off your pants your body was ..It was amazing! You took me in your arms, you took me to the bedroom, I stood there watching you put candles and light them. Then you came from behind me and hugged me, kissed my neck and face, taking off my clothes slowly, your smell, your warm body ooo my love… of course I will not tell her all that.

Antigone - I came; I hope I was not gone too long.

Her - No, I was just looking outside.

Antigone - Let's start, I hope you feel more comfortable now

Her - Lets start. Where were we? (She went and sat in the armchair, she wanted to say it all and end this affair.)

Antigone -You described to me the changes in your life, your first job ...

Her - Oh yes, so out of nowhere, another dream came true and the book was being prepared, I did the lessons. Within 2.5 weeks my salary was very good, I was so happy. Suddenly one day he told me he wanted to take me to a party, he took me to a store where he bought me a very formal dress and all the accessories. Clothes that I would wear for the first time in my life! The next day we went, I did not know where we were going but I followed him. We arrived at a house that although it was not a mansion but it was not poor either. We entered and saw people completely unknown and of high society. I would like to disappear but I was there already I felt uncomfortable and of course, I told him. It was the first and last time I went to something like that. Maybe he understood that I would understand who he was by going to party like that, maybe I would become a target, I do not know what he may been thinking but he never ask me to go to something like that ever again. I preferred the way we were, low profile. We went out with people from my work and with a few select friends. No bodyguards had appeared in our lives while we were together.

Of course, it was not the only thing that had happened at the end of the month, I finally saw news and it showed the place where I had seen the car. I recognized the place and heard them say if anyone saw anything suspicious, whatever it was to report it to the phone they were showing. As a good citizen, I thought of calling and I was asked to go there. They told me where I had to go and I told them that I did not know where this place was and they suggested that someone come and pick me up. I was going to work so I told them if they could come and be in front of the cafeteria so I would not be late at work. Meeting them so near at work it will be easy for me. I was ashamed to tell him. Maybe he would tell me that all this was nonsense. I did not consider it that my information was worth it. That's why I felt ashamed of telling him about it. So two men came to the appointment, we sat down, we each order something and I explained to them what had happened, about the car and the license plate. They thanked me and left, after two or three days they informed me that my information had helped them unimaginably. Of course, he had learned the same day of my meeting with the police. He had asked me in a sad manner, of course, I was surprised, but I replied to him that it was probably something not important and that my info are stupid.

Antigone - Did not he ask you for details?

Her - No, I did not tell him anything, nor later when I was told how useful my information was, so many changes were happening in my life ....!

Antigone - How did your relationship continue?

Her - In a fast pace. My parents did not know about this relationship. I did not want them to think that it was all because of him. My dreams were coming true. One day he came and asked me to put on comfortable pants and sneakers, warm and comfortable clothes. I asked him in vain in a playful style, he did not tell me where he was taking me; all he told me was that it was worth the surprise. I told him that I had left a lot of work behind me and he just smiled. I finally found myself taking riding lessons! How I wanted to learn riding! Therefore, he went on making me more surprising lessons on all the things I dreamed of doing! Dance classes, martial arts and so many more and he always came with me to everything! We were doing them together. At some point, he began to use the power he had. The unforgettable very luxuries trips began .....

Antigone - what kind of trips?

Her - We were going from one end of the earth to the other with private jets, expensive cars, deserted villas, well hidden in nature and by the locals themselves..I did scuba diving in dreamy areas and it was very expensive. From the paradise of exotic islands with unique beaches to huts and luxury ski hotels.

At first, I believed what he had told me, travel would fill my mind with experiences for new stories, as it would show me that there is mythical places in the world. That's the reason for taking me to those trips. I wrote throughout the travels. However, later he was all agony and sadness, when he thought I was not near him he took a look of sadness. I felt that he was in a hurry to give me as much happiness as possible. Even at night, he stayed awake and looked at me! I happened to wake up a few times and saw him looking at me wanting to remember me fill his soul of me as much as he could.

Antigone - How long had it been since you were together?

Her - I do not know the dates, all spring, all summer and until the end of September. I could feel he was hiding something from me. I kept asking him where did he find the money to pay for all that and why did we continue the trips since he was not happy....

Antigone - And did he answer you?

Her - Nothing, it changed the conversation but he knew I was not stupid.

Antigone - When you went to the villas how was it? Where were you?

 (She does not answer immediately pretending to try to remember.)I am not going to reveal such details, no; after all, I am saying from the beginning that I do not remember dates. She looks at the wall where there was nothing hanging and then another thought came to her. Are they watching me? Is it someone next door looking at me and hearing me? ....

Antigone - What's going on; Why did you stop; Your gaze ...

Her - My gaze, I was just surprised because while I was trying to remember, a thought came to me, that maybe they were watching me from somewhere without me realizing it.

Antigone - Of course not.

Her - If there were, would you tell me? No, do not answer it does not matter.

Antigone - You do not trust me, it's natural.

Her - I do not know many details about the trips, because I did not imagine that I would need to know. Besides, I did not ask because everything was a fairytale for me. Everything was done fast and by private means. I did not want to look ungrateful but I was not interested either, I was living every moment to the fullest. I was not born rich and with this kind of treatment to analyze it. I was in constant shock from one surprise to another; I was living in a dream! Would you spoil the dream if you were in my position with the risk of waking up or would you live it for as long as it lasted? Besides, I was sure that it would end on its own, why bring the end faster .... .Suddenly dreams and premonitions began .... A! I forgot to tell you about this. Well, I always learned about them a few hours before leaving. I had as much time as I needed to pack my bags. He would come to the hotel room or the house and tell me to pack my bags because in three hours at most we would leave for another surprise he had for me..

Antigone - So you did not always live in secluded houses but also went to hotels?

Her - Yes, in the beginning when he took me to the islands we used to go by jet from one airport to another for refueling. He did not want cruises because as he said it would take us so much time to arrive and we will have to go to places that he did not consider the places a cruise offers would be notably. It took me as he said in places privately that few could afford to admire. As soon as we arrived, a luxurious and fast car was always waiting for us. I remember we were in the car for about an hour or two, passing the village or the small town, but never big cities and it led to roads where there was only nature. Sometimes a cliff overlooking the sea, small roads, sometimes forest, plains and in the end always a house big or small but a deserted place with or without private beaches. With a large swimming pool overlooking the whole place or with fairytale private beaches. Most of the time a trusted person was waiting for us who took care of the place or for everything to just be ready for us. Even the man who was there when I asked him, the hours he was asleep, when I asked him if others were staying, if it was his or not or if he just rented it to rich people ,nothing, I was not learning anything. He politely rejected me and without me realizing it, the discussion changed. We were not always alone on the beaches; one or two people appeared as bodyguards.

Antigone - You said something about dreams before.

Her - Yes. They were warnings from myself. I felt that something was happening. At first, I did not say anything, he saw me becoming more and more anxious and thoughtful, But then I was waking up from the dreams I was anxious and scared. The joy from my eyes was gone. He would ask me and I would explain to him, he would hold me in his arms saying that he loves me and I will never be in any danger. When suddenly I felt my instinct awaken, I started talking to him about the trips we made and arguing. I shouted challenging him to tell me the truth about whether he had used all those places with many others like me. Asking him if those places are his or not. Challenging him to tell me something. I knew he was hiding something from me, I was feeling like he was running away than going on trips with me. He was on edge all the time at our last trips. I try asking him polite but nothing so I try to make him tell me.

Her - Why don't you tell me if they rent them to others, maybe because you went there many times before me with many women!

Him - What got in to you? Why are you acting like this?

Her - I am leaving!........................ I opened the door and left, I felt a sadness, a desire to escape. I knew I was not saying it out of jealousy, but because I wanted to make him tell me the truth of what was going on and why hide the fact if those places were his or of friends of his. I left and went for a long walk alone and I ate out alone. I sat for coffee and watched people pass by and that was helping me calm down. Until he found me, he was terrified that I left him. He was telling me how scared he is and never to do it again. I ask him why he feels so scared but nothing. Maybe I felt like it was time to leave him, I felt so alive when I was alone, so strong and so independent maybe I was tired of being scared, feeling like something was wrong and maybe I was involved somewhere bad. Those places in order to have all that money what kind of a job he was doing. When I was with him, I felt all those feelings growing up. All those questions. I was lost in my thoughts and I saw myself running away. Mistakes began to happen. My behavior was working. He did not want us to return. He once told me in fear that they would separate us. I persuaded him to come back I condemned him! Of course, I did not knew it back then. When we returned only then I saw those two friends who were together in the beginning when I had first seen him. I also found his weapon forgotten in one of his jackets!

Antigone - What did you thought when you saw the gun?

Her - That he is involve in bad things! Oh, my god I was so scared! Maybe I was also involved! Then I remembered him telling me that I would not be harm in any way. That made me think that I am in danger for sure. He was involved with drugs, or with what? That's when I started keeping my distance from him and I was watching around me all the time. I was scared if he learned that I knew he was involved somewhere will I be in danger. I asked him if he needed to kill someone he loved he would do it or not and he told me he would rather kill himself.

Antigone - Did not suspect anything? Didn't he tell you anything?

Her - No, nothing. There was a party where he had to be, I had to work, I did not want to go alone after work and he had to go there sooner than I could. I did not want to go with those 'friends' of his and I asked him if a friend and colleague could accompany me. Therefore, we got dressed well and left, I went to work dressed like that. He had told me that if I did not want to be by his side he would not mind because it would be a chaos at that party after all. I was so happy hearing him say it! I was so afraid to be seen next to him and being a target of some kind! I stayed with Christos the colleague. We had a great time, we danced ……. He did not stop looking at me, he was definitely jealous. With Christos, I felt safe again after such a long time.

Antigone - Christos ………

Her - He is a very good friend even now; he stood by me, even that night. He realized that most of the people there were not 'good guys' and he told me. He asked me to leave and I accepted. I had not even thought for a moment when I ask him to come with me where I was taking him! It was so selfish of me I know now. He could have think the worst for me after being there….I ask a waiter to tell us how we could leave and we started looking for a way out. The place was huge. We passed rooms one after another full of people; he was holding my hand because we almost got lost among ourselves in such a huge crowd. As we opened another door in our quest to find a way to leave faster, we saw people taking drugs and having sex orgies. Out of our terror, Christos grabbed my hand and we started running without knowing where to go. The laughter left us and we were afraid that they would consider us witnesses. I had completely forgotten that he could provide us with protection. I vaguely remember that as we were running up the stairs to a balcony, when we came out on a balcony I think I saw him looking at us in surprise, I think he ran to find us ………. I was blurred, we had finally found ourselves somewhere dark and quiet, to the garage, a tear left and Christos wiped it. Our hearts were trembling for a moment, we stopped and went down the stairs when we saw the yard with the cars we felt relief. We ran to the car and passed in front of a car with the license plates I had seen and reported. My blood stopped. Christos turned and pulled me to leave, we got in the car and left. I remember I was boneless, motionless. I could not move or breathe.

< Christos > Calm down, we left, no one is chased us. (He touched me with his hand and I looked at him crying and trembling. We went to his house) Why are you trembling?

- I want to change clothes, can I stay here?

< Christos > But of course. I will bring you my own clothes to put on, a uniform. (I remained motionless a tangle on the couch). Come go straight in and change I left them on the bed. (I went embarrassed, changed and sat back on the couch with my feet up to hold them with my hands) I made you hot chocolate that you like so much, do not be afraid (I was shocked, he hug me)

-Don't leave me alone! Please! I told him.

That's how I fell asleep. Terrified I woke up in the early hours of the morning I saw him sleeping next to me and I fell asleep again. He did not ask me how I knew them or how I was at this party as a guest. In the morning when I woke up he had made breakfast, the smells… .I probably was very hungry. I had forgotten for a while, he even bought me specific wipes to wash off my make up! When I went to the bathroom, I saw a note: "use the toothbrush I got for you and I got you wipes for your makeup" I smiled. I went to the kitchen for breakfast, but as I was eating, my mind was elsewhere. Christos had understood that something else must have scared me, something I had seen while he did not.

< Christos > What else have you seen that scared you so much?

- E, sorry, I don't remember!! Shit I honest do not remember!! All I remember is the fear I felt!

< Christos > Maybe you have erased it from your memory. If you want to know what it was, I have a friend that does hypnotherapy.

- Yes let's go now, ah, no I have no clothes and I do not want to go home.

< Christos > I'm going to buy you a pair of jeans and a blouse from across the street.

-No, I do not want to be alone let me try to put something of yours. Do not answer let the phone ring please. He went next to his neighbor and friend and asked her for a pair of jeans, he asked her not to tell anyone that she saw him and that he would explain to her later. We got dressed and left

< Christos > Here we are, let's go up… ..thank god you are here! Are you waiting for an appointment? I need your help. I want to help my friend, yesterday she had an experience in which she saw something that terrified her and she cannot remember it. She is left with the fear that she saw something terrible.

<Y> Well, sit here comfortably as for you, you can stay without making any noise. Have you done anything like this before?

- I have but not heavy hypnosis.

<Y> Okay, I'm going to ask you to look at this pendulum and give you instructions. You feel your eyes so heavy…………………………………… Go back to last night and remember where you are, go to the party, tell me what do you see (Christos whispered to her where we

were)…………………………………………… *if you do not want to say it , it does not matter as long as you see it and when I wake you, you will remember it all. Do not be afraid, you are not in danger now, calm down ………… ..When you have seen what you do not remember you will be able to open your eyes………………………………….*

Her - That way I remembered what I had seen that night. When I opened my eyes, I started to cry. Christos tried to calm me down and I asked him to take me to his house. On the way I was silent and I asked him to finally take me to a hotel, he would not find me there I told him. He stated a fake name and paid, in a simple hotel. As I had asked him.

Antigone - Didn't he look for you?

Her - But of course! However, I did not pick up his calls. He went up to the room with me and we had the following conversation

< Christos > Tell me, what did you see, what is happening to you, please?

- It cannot happen! Oh my god! I have to think, calm down. I was right about the bad feeling. The dream is over!

< Christos > What dream?

- If I tell you I will be putting you in danger too, I want to think, but if he finds you he will force you to tell him where I am.

< Christos > If you need me I can stay.

- No, I have to be alone so I can think. Sorry for everything I should not have put you in to all this. I will call you I promise ………

Her - He left. I sat in the armchair and I saw my happiness flowing through my hands and leaving. I closed my eyes with my hands and I saw again my gaze falling on the car of that night. Inside it had the reflection of the little light on an object and made it to stand out. That's how I noticed it! A golden cigar case; not just any one but the one I gave him on one of our trips. Expensive and unique, special order just for him! The special size of the special minutes of cigars with the words I had requested engraved on it. There was no way it was someone else's you know. I felt like I was dying! I wanted to be in a room that I could break what I could find until the anger I felt was gone.

Antigone - But you still did not know the truth, when did he found you,….

Her - No, I did not knew the whole truth, but the female intuition knew the killer, she knew that he was her boyfriend. I thought he was involved but not to what extent. I could not imagine such an end, nor can I now. I believed that if we ever broke up we would go on with our lives as friends and not him in a prison! A life in prison, and to do what! Should I go see him? Should I tell him what? Should I give him false hopes?

Antigone - But if he could get out of prison what then?...

Her - If.... no! If he manage to leave from this country, another would look for him; so many people will want revenge. I do not want such a life. No! You cannot understand what I felt back then. He was looking for me. He went to my job and talked to Christos, asked him what happened that night. Because he saw us so frightened. He asked some of the people that were at that party that night after seeing us running so scared if they have seen us or what have happened but no one knew anything. Therefore, they did not understand from all that drugs in their system that some had opened the door for a while. Christos explained to him what we had seen and that I was very upset but he had not seen me, I had disappeared.

Antigone - How did he felt?

Her - Terror, he was as scared as he never ever felt before in his life that's what he said when I met him and saw the terror in his eyes. As I was saying, I stayed there crying. When I opened the door, it was a girl from the hotel asking me if I was hungry or if I wanted something. I replied that today my heart was broken, that it was impossible for me to be hungry. All I want is to cry because my heart hurts. I will not harm myself; I just want to cry alone. She looked at me and nodded that she understood. She would make sure no one bothered me, but she would leave something light like snacks outside the door for when or if I will be, hungry and she left. I closed the door and lay down on the bed, the curtains were open and it was starting to rain. I watched the heavy rain, it always made me feel good to see and hear the heavy rain when my heart was in pain. I approached the window and sat there curled up crying and looking at the raindrops on the glass and my mind was starting to empty of thoughts. I just felt the pain, the sadness, the loneliness. No such end no! This was hurting me the most. The night came and I was there watching the rain. I did not want to go anywhere, just stay there, I was not afraid that he would hurt me, that fear was gone. Logic began to come; the rain had done its miracle. Even though the tears were still running, I could think logically. In addition, the pain had to manifest. I had to see him and no matter how I would chose to tell him, the only sure thing was that I had to go to the police. I was sure of that. However, how would I do it? Should I talk to him first? What should I do? How do you know what is the most correct way to do it?

Antigone - Have, you ever wondered if he was innocent?

Her - No! My instinct did not let me. He was definitely involved. I called the police asking for the police officer who had the case. I asked him to come. It was not long before he appeared. I opened the door and did not let him tell me anything. I told him "come on, don't ask anything, just hear what I have to say. He sat on the armchair and I in my corner, near the window down on the floor. He took a pillow and his jacket and approached me, looking scared at how I was. I was ready to collapse. He asked me to sit on the pillow and I was embarrassed so I did it without looking at him. He covered me with his jacket without saying anything else and sat down on the armchair. I looked at him and he was looking at me with such tenderness and fear that he would upset me and if he did, I would faint or worst. I started talking to him: "We saw each other again... .. Fortunately, it is raining so hard otherwise, my heart would have exploded. If I cry I apologize (he grimaced that it did not bother him) I called you here to ask you a lot... .. Just tell me with a yes or a no please, the truth... .. (I cried) the victims were many from the cold killer that you are looking? I thought so! Were they also good people? Do not be afraid to tell me the truth I can take it.

-       Yes, they were not criminals or drug lords. Ordinary people, who got in the way of their bosses' dirty plans or competitors with families, children. They pay him to kill them, maybe they saw something they shouldn't, they couldn't buy off their silence or they were in the wrong place at the wrong time.

-       I read somewhere that some were older people.

-       Yes.

-       A ruthless killer who protected the bad guys or did it just for the money, right?

-       Maybe, I don't know.

-       O! Believe me for the money and the good life!

\-   *What is happening to you? Were you threatened? Do you know something?*

\-   *If I tell you... and you understand the rest but I do not tell you the whole truth will you, let me have the opportunity to call you when I will be ready?*

\-   *I don't understand you..*

\-   *If I know someone who can tell you what you need so you can catch him, will you let me tell you his name whenever I'm ready?.....I lost my whole life today you know.... (he came and hugged me)*

\-   *My little one, I have never seen anyone suffer as much as you and that tear my soul.*

\-   *Do I look so bad? My soul you know has countless bloody wounds! I will hand him over to you even if I die by doing so, I am in shock you know but I will do the right thing but I need a few more days. Please, I am hiding from those I love because one of them is the person you are looking for. I have to betray someone, how can you do such a thing? It's my first time you know.*

\-   *You cannot, I appreciate your honesty, I respect your courage and I believe you will do the right thing. Well, OK! You need something; I cannot leave you like that.*

\-   *- I'm strong, I just need to mourn and recover.*

Antigone - You know, the police officer told us, you were ready to have a heart attack. You were so pale. He was afraid that if he pressured you to say what you could not, you would die at that moment. He was very scared; he did not want to be responsible for your death. You felt a lot of pain and he wondered if he would have the courage to do what you did.

Her -I was not ready to meet him, you know, but I knew I did not have much time. Nor could I bear not to hand him over to the police. However, I loved him so much! I wiped my tears, washed my face and called him overnight. Let's meet, I told him, I would come in the morning there. He was asking me where I was, he was crazy worried. I listened to him and I was about to lose my courage, my logic, my composure. I will come tomorrow I told him and I ended the call. I fell asleep from crying and in the morning, I woke up from the knock on the door. I got up from the bed where I slept with my clothes and shoes, I opened it and it was Christos. "I couldn't stand it, I had to see you, to see if you are ok" he told me. I fell into his arms and cried for a while until I looked at him and told him I had to stop crying. "Yes you have to. Whatever has happened or will happen I want you to know I will be by your side! He looked me in the eyes; he meant them, everything he just said to me! I needed somewhere to tell what had happened to me and so I told him: I want to tell you the whole truth without much detail because I have to leave. ..That night in the parking lot, the first car we saw was the one the police were looking for the cold killer-executor. Inside the car, I saw something that is a unique object and I gave it to the man I love. Do you understand?! The man who changed my life for the better is mixed up with that, whatever his role... ..I talked to the police and I told them what I saw no matter how much I am dyeing inside form pain. But now I have to go home and meet him, I do not know what I will tell him, I love him and I have to find the strength to turn him in .... The bewildered poor man sat on the edge of the bed and put his hands on his face saying "My God! How is that possible! How will you endure it ?! I could not, I knew him a little, I knew a murderer... »I did not let him take me home; I did not want him to see us and break his heart making him jealous. Christos was afraid to let me go alone, I told him that I would inform him, I would have my mobile phone open. I was sure he would not hurt me. The police officer followed me to the house without me seeing him. I arrived home by taxi; he heard the taxi and saw him looking out the window. He had come down the stairs and he hugged me overtaken me at the entrance, with his slippers obviously on looking so upset. The porter looked at us.

Antigone - How did you feel when you saw him?

Her - I had forgotten the reason I was there .... He hugged me tightly, kissed me and I melted from his love for me. No, I was wrong! I wanted to believe I was wrong... ..I told him to go upstairs and I was left in his arms. When we entered our apartment, he walked away from me, went to the center of the living room and looked at me. He asked me with the fear painted on his face if I was well and why I had not called him earlier, I knew he would protect me, he told me. You were afraid of me, he asked me. What I had seen that night and him seeing the fear in my eyes! He was afraid I was afraid of him. God I love you! Over my own life! He screamed. I know I told him, I know you would never do me any harm, but you did it without wanting to. He remained speechless. And I went on, why did you hide from me the real world you live in? Why did you let me love you so much and then show me the scary world you live in ?! You know that I would not accept being with someone like you as much as I loved you, I would have left! You know that!!! I said angrily to him, and yet you did it, you hid the truth from me, you did not tell me from the beginning, the tears started to flow and he started crying with fear, do not approach me, tell me why, I loved another person not who you truly are !?Why you let me love you???? Why??? And he said to me, "I apologize! You are right! You will leave;" "I cannot see you crying I told him and I opened my arms, he came in my hug crying and I whispered to him, "you knew we would break up, why did not you tell me? I would have been prepared; I would have made my choices. While now ……….. I do not hold a grudge against you I love you…."

He understood that I was leaving; I did not have to tell him. I had wanted him so much, without thinking; I started kissing him pulling his face towards me. I surprised him; maybe he thought for a while that I would not leave. He got up and I started… .. we made love for the last time that's how I wanted to remember him. When it was over and I realized that, I had to tell him. A tear went away, I got up I dressed silently, and he looked at me and said, "It's something more serious right? My God ?! ". "I want to remember us as before when you made love to me and I hope one day you will forgive me. I love you do not dispute me! One day I will be able to forget the pain you caused me by making me choose. Are you the cold-blooded killer? I told him «E! How …… ..does not matter, God what have I done, you learned it and you were tortured! My baby, I'm sorry I did not want to hurt you "He jumped out of bed, I looked at him with pain in my eyes and he knelt down, grabbed me by my legs and constantly apologized to me. Then I said to him "I could not write off the innocent victims from my mind for a love! How could you do such a thing! If we made a family… I do not want to think about it, I am leaving. !". "For God shake what have I done to you!! I would never hurt you! I see in your eyes shame for me and you doubt me. I wish I did not live to see this! Not this! I would never hurt you! Believe me! My God, you were afraid of me and that's why you were hiding….". He was standing there crying, apologizing; I could not bear to see him. I loved him you see. I ran away, I came out crying and there, there were the police officer and Christos waiting for me

to my great surprise. Going out I saw them sitting outside their cars, surprise and shame that's what I felt seeing them both there.
Antigone - Shame why?
Her - But I made love to him; the time was past, early in the morning. They must have understood that.
Antigone - The police officer told us he was there because he knew you were going to go to the one he thought was involved and maybe put your life in danger. There he suddenly saw Christos arriving, approached him and asked him why he was there and who he was. Christos after his surprise, told him that he was worried about you and that he is a friend and the policeman replied that he was worried too because you were definitely with a dangerous man. In their statements, they also said that they saw you coming out as chased, pale, crying.
Her - I was relieved to see them there. I looked at the police officer and said, "How right am I now to betray the one I love the most?". He told me "My dear child it was matter of hours to find him .He did not run away or try to leave the country. He stayed here because he definitely wanted us to catch him. All the organization months now, we caught them one by one from your information. He returned to the country, maybe he wanted to change even at the last minute. You will get over it because you have people who care for you." and showed me Christos. From whom I asked him to take me away not to see his arrest. Suddenly two cars and security men appeared. I looked again at our apartment and left ……. .. I learned that he did not show any resistance he was waiting for them.
Antigone - Would you like to know his testimony? I talked to him about what happened, about his feelings for you. He did not accuse you of anything, he thinks you did the right thing; I can let you read what he said.
Her - I would love that. Thank you.
Antigone - Here it's all, I'll leave you alone, when you're done leave it on my desk and you can leave. The police officer who is outside will lead you to the exit.
(She opened the door and left, telling the police officer to leave her alone for a while and show her the way out. He asked: "What is your opinion?" "Niko she is innocent, I would never want to be in her place! It takes lots of guts to do what she did! She will find the strength to overcome it!»)

…………...Please do not hurt her, I do not want her to suffer any more. I did not told her who I was, she loved me and I loved her. I wanted you to catch me because every time I looked into her innocent eyes every time she told me about the injustices of life, how much she wanted to be able to help people I felt disgraceful about myself. I hated me! I wanted to make her happy, to protect her and yet I hurt her. God, how she must be feeling and when she found out who I am! I was sure that she must have been suspected something, but I managed to direct her questions, to change the subject. I tried to leave her but I could not, I behaved so selfishly. She must hate me! Whatever happens, whatever happens to me I do not care anymore! I deserve it, tell me how is she, how did she get all of this? " . "She is strong she is hand in there!". "Does she hate me?". "No! that's what she told us, she does not blame you, she owes you her life." "Tell her I really loved her. I will not forget what we experienced. I did not blame her, it needs guts to do what she did, and she would be eaten by guilt if she did not turn me in. Now she can find her peace and overcome me. She did the right thing, she changed me, her love, I had not killed anyone while we were together I could not have been next to her otherwise. Nothing had scared me in my life except that night I was looking for her. The fear and pain I feel is my greatest punishment. That night when she told me that she knows… .I saw the pain in her eyes and I felt my soul become a thousand pieces. The fear that I ruined her life …… the pain in my heart will never go away, someone else will make her happy and truly love him and I will know that I lost what was most precious in my life. It's like ripping my soul…………...

Her - I cannot go on anymore, now I know at least that he does not hate me for betraying him while he had given me so much. You know I do not hate you, I know you are in pain and you deserve it. Our love was true but not the only one. I do not want to see you again; I want to live my life, to forget you. You changed my life I changed your life now I have to move on. I know that what I said was recorded so please I want you to tell him all that I just said…………….

-E! Sir what are you doing it here? Who are you?

- My name is Christos and I came to wait for her to come out ……………..

………………………(She had left the room and the police officer silently pointed her out. they finally reached the exit)
- Christos!! What are you doing here….
- I came to pick you up, I knew you would not want to be alone ………………………

Thank you for taking the time to read one more of my stories. I hope you enjoy it even if this one is a small one.